FANNY'S SISTER

Penelope Lively

FANNY'S SISTER

illustrated by Anita Lobel

E. P. DUTTON NEW YORK

The text was first published in 1976
by William Heinemann Ltd., London, England.

Library of Congress Cataloging in Publication Data

Lively, Penelope, date   Fanny's sister.

SUMMARY: Because she is afraid God will answer her prayer and
take her new baby sister back to heaven, nine-year-old
Fanny runs away from her home in England.
[1. Babies—Fiction.   2. Brothers and sisters—Fiction.
3. Runaways—Fiction] I. Lobel, Anita. II. Title.
PZ7.L7397Fan   [Fic]   79-20118   ISBN: 0-525-29618-2

Published in the United States by E. P. Dutton, a Division
of Elsevier-Dutton Publishing Company, Inc., New York

Designer: Riki Levinson

Printed in the U.S.A.   First Edition
10 9 8 7 6 5 4 3 2 1

to Sophie and Emma

FANNY DREAMED THAT A CAT was mewing out-side her door. "Be quiet," she said to it crossly, in her sleep, "be quiet or you'll wake me up." The dream dis-solved and she woke, warmly buried in her own bed, with a bright crack of light down the middle of the curtains telling her that it was morning. Outside, the milkman's pony clopped along the road, and a voice (Cook's, it must be, or Nellie the kitchen maid's per-haps) called out to him from the back door.

And something was mewing. But not a cat. Fanny sat bolt upright in bed, and listened. She knew that noise. It was the noise that started up afresh, next door in the nursery, as regularly, it seemed to Fanny, as Christmas and Easter and birthdays. Last year when she was eight and the year before when she was seven and the year before . . . well, nearly every year anyway, because Fanny was the eldest and then there were Albert and Emma and Harriet and Charles and Jane and Susan.

It was the noise of a new baby. A brand-new, just-born baby. In there, thought Fanny, sitting up in bed freezing in her flannel nightie, and glaring at the closed door between the night-nursery and the day-nursery, in there, tucked up in the cradle, was a new baby, red of face and loud of voice. Mamma, who had been not-very-well for weeks and weeks so that you must not jump and shout on the stairs, would be lying pale and smiling in the big bed, and presently Fanny and Albert and all the others would be taken in one by one to say good morning in hushed voices and give her one quiet and gentle kiss before they went away again. And in the nursery there would be that mewing noise, night and day, with Nurse all cross and busy at the washing steaming in front of the fire, and no time for stories after tea. Her huge, white-aproned lap would be occupied by the new baby, as it had been occupied by last year's baby (Susan) and the baby of the year before that and the year before that.

Once upon a time, a long time ago, in a time that seemed all golden and glorious, like pictures of Heaven in Fanny's Bible, that lap had been Fanny's place. There she had sat and listened to stories and had squares of hot buttered toast popped into her mouth. And then there had come Albert and the lap had been only partly hers, and then Emma and it was no longer hers at all, and presently she found herself pushed upwards into the schoolroom, to Miss Purser with her rabbity teeth and her ruler that tapped your knuckles if you did not pay attention, and her horrible, horrible sums.

"I hate babies," said Fanny to the picture of an angel on the wall at the foot of her bed. And the angel, its halo exploding into a fiery sky, stared disapprovingly back, because nice little girls do not hate anything, least of all their dear little brothers and sisters.

The door opened. The hump of bedclothes in the next bed that was Emma sat up and said she was hungry for breakfast.

"All in good time," said Nurse. She drew the curtains and light came into the room, and a blackbird's song, and the church bells ringing. It must be Sunday, thought Fanny, and alongside the crossness that the mewing noise had brought came a further crossness

at the thought of Sunday. Sunday meant church, and learning by heart a passage from the Bible, and no noisy games, and more church, and repeating the passage from the Bible to Papa in his study. "I hate Sunday," said Fanny to the angel, and the angel raised its eyes to the fiery sky in horror and disbelief.

Now everybody was awake. Susan began to cry, and Nurse picked her up and started to dress her. "Come along now, Fanny," she said, "up you get. Don't you want to see what a nice surprise there is for you in the nursery?"

No, said Fanny silently.

"I know," said Albert, "there is a new baby. The new baby has come. Is it a boy or a girl?"

"A lovely little girl," said Nurse. She put Susan on the floor to crawl around, and set about brushing Harriet's hair, briskly, taking no notice of Harriet's loud protesting noises. "A little sister for you."

"Hurray!" said Emma, and Albert groaned theatrically until Nurse snapped at him to be quiet.

"Did God send the new baby?" said Harriet, wriggling under the hairbrush.

Nurse said yes, God sent the new baby and in church today they must all say thank you to Him. "What's

5

the matter with you, Fanny?" she went on, whipping clothes out of drawers. "Get up and put on your Sunday dress."

"I feel ill," said Fanny. "I have . . . I have a stomachache. And my throat is sore. And my legs hurt," she added. If you were going to do a thing you might as well do it properly. Nurse herself said that, almost every day.

"Let me see your tongue," said Nurse. And then, "Get up this minute. I never heard such nonsense."

Fanny got up, scowling, and scowled her way into her tight, stiff, Sunday dress and boots, and then into the nursery where Sukie the nursery maid was ladling porridge into bowls. In the cradle by the fire the new baby mewed, and Nurse picked it up and talked to it and then took it away downstairs to Mamma. Fanny burned her tongue on her porridge and kicked Albert under the table, half by accident and half on purpose, so that Albert kicked back and there was a fight. When Nurse returned, Albert was sent to stand in one corner of the room and Fanny in the other.

"Birds in their little nests agree," said Nurse. "You can stop there now, the pair of you, till I say." And Fanny, staring sullenly at the wallpaper, thought that

Nurse couldn't know all that much about birds. What about baby cuckoos, she thought? They push all the other little birds out so that there's only them left. Clever cuckoos, she said to herself. Behind her, at the table, last year's baby (Susan) spattered her breakfast on the floor and howled.

Breakfast ended. Fanny and Albert were released from their corners. Nurse scolded them again and said that badly behaved children would not be allowed to go downstairs before church and see their Mamma. Then the Old Children (Fanny, Albert and Emma) were sent to the schoolroom to write out the Sunday text and learn it by heart to recite to Papa, while the Young Children (all the rest) were taken off by Sukie to be cleaned and put into outdoor clothes and packed into the donkey cart for an airing. Fanny wished, and not for the first time, that she was still one of the Young Children.

In the schoolroom, a bluebottle, trapped like Fanny, buzzed fretfully against the window. Fanny opened her exercise book and wrote the date at the top of a clean page: Sunday, 6 September 1865. In the middle of the green baize tablecloth was a sheet of paper on which Papa had written in his neat sloping handwriting the verses from the Bible that they were to copy out and learn. Fanny began to write, in her not-so-neat writing ". . . And God said unto them, Be fruitful, and multiply, and replenish the earth." It was all about Adam and Eve, this bit. God was telling them what they were to do and what they weren't to do. Fanny knew what multiply meant, because of Miss Purser and her horrible sums. That is what we are doing, too, she thought, being fruitful and multiplying, because there is a new baby every year. God must think we are a nice obedient family.

She looked balefully out of the window down into the street outside the house, where she could see Hobbs the groom standing beside the donkey cart, holding the donkey while the Young Children were loaded into the cart, two at each side. They all looked happy and excited, and Fanny, watching them, remembered what it used to feel like jogging down the lanes, holding on to the wooden sides of the donkey cart with both hands, while Nurse led the donkey and the donkey's furry ears twitched against the flies. It's not fair, thought Fanny in a rage, it just isn't fair.

Dust spun in a shaft of sunshine. Albert sighed and grunted as he wrote, the tip of his tongue sticking out

between his teeth. Emma ground her boots maddeningly upon the leg of her chair and muttered as she learned by heart. Fanny said to herself, over and over again, "And God saw everything he had made, and behold it was very good," and thought gloomily that she would never know this to say to Papa tonight. She would stammer and stutter and stop, and Papa would be displeased and it would not be good at all.

At last Nurse came to fetch them to get ready for church. When they were washed and brushed, they went down into the hall to wait for Papa to come from his study and take them to see Mamma. Fanny, her hands clasped inside her fur muff (she liked her Sunday muff, it was the only thing that was agreeable about Sundays), heard the door open on the floor above and his footsteps coming down the stairs, and then there was his large, black figure above her, complete with shiny black Sunday hat, and the gold watch-chain stretched across his waistcoat. When she was very young, she had longed to pull that watch-chain but had never dared, because Papa was not the kind of person to whom you could ever, ever do such a thing. Fanny loved her father, and she thought him extremely grand and important, but he seemed somehow very far away,

even though she lived in the same house with him and always had done. Loving him was more like loving God or the Queen than loving, for instance, Nurse, or Jupiter the sheep dog or the donkey or even Mamma, who was also grand and a little far away but not nearly so far away as Papa.

Mamma, this morning, lay in bed in the big bedroom like a piece of precious china cocooned in tissue paper. She smiled and kissed each of them and asked what they thought of their new little sister. Emma said that she was nice, and Albert said that she was nice but it was a pity she had not been a boy.

"Come now, Fanny," said Papa, "have you lost your tongue? What do you think?"

"She makes a lot of noise," said Fanny in a sullen voice, and Mamma and Papa both laughed and said that all babies cry and that was perfectly natural. Outside, the church bells were ringing, which made Papa take his watch from his waistcoat pocket and say that it was time to go.

Walking to church, Fanny forgot her irritation about the new baby. There was a dogfight at the end of their street, which was exciting and interesting, and blackberries to pick in the hedge along the

lane (quickly, behind Papa's back, cramming them
into her mouth before he could see), and her best
enemy, Clara Binns, the doctor's daughter, outside
the church gates. Fanny and Clara stuck out their
tongues at each other, as far as they would go, while
Papa removed his hat to Mrs. Binns and Mrs. Binns
inquired after Mamma and sent effusive messages of
congratulations and affection.

"Shall I say thank you to God for the new baby,
Papa?" said Emma, and Papa smiled and patted
Emma's head and said yes, that would be very nice.
And all Fanny's crossness came flowing back.

Kneeling in their pew, Fanny stared through a crack
in her fingers at the Sunday bonnet of Mrs. Binns in
front of her (a new bonnet, with much in the way of
ribbons and flowers and fruit; a ridiculous bonnet, in
Fanny's opinion) and thought about God. She always imagined that God, if one ever saw Him, would
look rather like Papa, but in long flowing robes, like
people in the Bible, and even sterner.

She began to pray. First she thought of all the
things she had done wrong since last Sunday and
said she was sorry about them. I am sorry, she said
silently, that I pinched Emma (but it was because

she spoiled my book so I hope she is saying she is sorry to You, too) and I am sorry I wouldn't eat my rice pudding (but You created rice pudding, which is a pity, and if You had not I wouldn't have to eat it) and I am sorry I was rude to Nurse. She paused to try to remember if there was anything she had left out, as God would know anyway, since He was supposed to know everything. And anything that I have forgotten, she added. And please make me good. She always asked this. And it seemed to her that God was not being very successful. But perhaps in her case it was a great deal more difficult than in most and was just taking longer.

A fly settled on the bunch of cherries at the side of Mrs. Binns' bonnet, apparently deceived by their natural appearance. Fanny watched it with interest until it flew away, and the cherries made her think of cherry tart. Her mouth watered. She dearly loved cherry tart. Cherry tart with a great deal of clotted cream. And it had not appeared upon the dinner table for a very long time now. Months and months. Years, even.

Please, said Fanny to God, please may we have cherry tart for dinner today. From time to time she

asked God for small things like this. She had never asked for anything large, because she did not feel that she really deserved it, but small things, such as cherry tarts and a day with no sums to do, she felt could not be objected to. So far, God had never obliged (except just once, over a fine day for her birthday) and she assumed this was because she was so wicked. Cherry tart *and* clotted cream, she prayed. And thank you for sending the new baby, she added, unwillingly. Thank you for sending it even though I didn't ask for it, and in fact I wish You would take it back again.

There was a creaking and rustling as the Vicar took his place and everyone stood up to sing the first hymn. "Alleluia! Alleluia!" sang Fanny lustily, glad to get up off her knees. And in a sudden fit of well-being, she nudged Albert, who nudged her back until they were both quelled by a glance from Papa.

Fanny put on her most virtuous expression and gazed intently at Mr. Chubb, the Vicar, as though she were drinking in his every word. Mr. Chubb, she knew, could not see her, as he wore the thickest spectacles she had ever seen on anyone and was famous for never recognizing people. He had much offended her mamma once by mistaking her for Mrs. Hancock, the grocer's wife. Mamma was very much grander than a grocer's wife.

"Amen," sang Fanny loudly, and the Sunday service unrolled, as familiar in its progress as the rising and setting of the sun, until the Vicar pronounced the blessing and everybody filed out into the churchyard to bow and remove hats to one another.

They went home. Papa was in a most genial mood and allowed them to stop for a few minutes to throw stones into the village pond, and made no comment when Albert climbed upon the stone wall beside the lane and walked along it. Fanny wished that she could follow him but knew that what was allowed—at a pinch—to boys was certainly not allowed to a girl wearing her best Sunday dress and coat. She wished, also, and not for the first time, that she was a boy.

At home, the Young Children were just being unloaded from the donkey cart at the end of their outing. Fanny hugged the donkey, and the donkey, who never showed its feelings, except for a general impression of gloom and suffering, stood in resignation, its ears drooping, while she buried her face in the thick dusty fur of its neck.

The Young Children were taken up to the nursery while Fanny, Albert and Emma went with Papa into the dining room for Sunday dinner. One of the only things in favor of being an Older Child, Fanny considered, was that you were allowed into the dining room for Sunday dinner with the grown-ups. Not only did this make you feel interesting and important (even if you did have to pay more than usual attention to good manners), but the food was better. There was no tapioca or semolina, but things like roast beef and Yorkshire pudding. Fanny licked her lips in happy anticipation as she sat down in her place, hands neatly folded in her lap; lowered her head while Papa said grace; and raised it again as he picked up the carving knife to sharpen it. There was the most exquisite smell of roast lamb, and as the green baize door to the kitchen swung to and fro behind Mary the parlormaid, gusts of something else delicious that she could not for the moment recognize.

They ate. Papa asked them questions about what they had learned in the schoolroom with Miss Purser this week. He was still in a very good humor and only once told Albert to sit up straight and not speak with his mouth full. Fanny, agreeably stuffed with roast lamb, forgot most of her troubles, such as Miss Purser's sums and that passage from the Bible that she would certainly not be able to recite this evening, and chatted to Papa about one thing and another. The roast lamb was taken away to the kitchen, and Papa asked Mary to bring in the next course.

"Well, now," said Papa, removing the cover from a dish to release another gust of that pleasant smell that Fanny could not quite place, "what has Cook made for us today?" And his knife hovered over a golden and shining pastry surface. He cut a triangle from the pastry. "Ah! A cherry tart. Cherries and clotted cream. Fanny, will you have a helping of tart?"

Fanny stared at the tart and her eyes grew round with amazement. Cherry tart? Cherry tart *and* clotted cream? Was she hearing and seeing correctly? But yes, there indeed was the beautiful rosy gleam of cherries steaming beneath the pastry in a bath of thick sweet juice; and there indeed was the silver bowl piled high with yellow clotted cream, being placed by Mary at this very moment in the middle of the table. She had prayed for cherry tart, and lo! cherry tart had been granted to her.

Thank you, said Fanny fervently and silently, and held out her plate to Papa. And at the very same moment a thought struck her, with such suddenness and such effect that the plate quavered in her hand and would have dropped upon the table if Papa had not snatched it from her.

She had asked God for cherry tart. And then she had thanked Him for the new baby and wished that He would take it back again.

And He had granted the first part of her request.

"No!" said Fanny, out loud, in panic. "No! I didn't mean it. Please don't! I didn't really mean it at all!"

"Fanny!" said Papa crossly. "Whatever is the matter with you? Kindly pay attention to what you are doing. And what are you talking about? You didn't mean what?" He handed her plate back to her, piled high with glistening cherries, golden pastry and cream.

"Nothing," said Fanny, and hung her head over the cherries. She stuck her spoon into them and took a mouthful, and the cherries tasted of nothing at all

because her head was filled with a terrible picture of the new baby being swept up to Heaven, naked, with a little pair of wings on its back, like cherubs in the Bible. She put her spoon down again and stared miserably at the table. Everybody else ate their tarts and said they would like a second helping.

"Fanny!" said Papa sternly. "Mary is waiting to clear the plates. Eat up your tart at once, please."

Fanny took another mouthful and thought that she might be sick. The cherries were horribly sticky and sweet (how could she ever have liked them?) and the cream full of nasty lumps. With tears in her eyes she crammed spoonful after spoonful into her mouth. Albert and Emma sat staring at her in surprise while Papa, tall and black-clothed and awesome, gazed at the window as though she were not there. Dining-room manners did not allow that food should be left uneaten on a plate. Neither, for that matter, did nursery manners, but in the nursery there was the ever open mouth of Sam, the nursery dog, beneath the table.

At last the plate was empty. Papa said grace again and the children were free to go.

"What's the matter?" whispered Albert on the

stairs. "Have you got a stomachache?" Fanny scowled at him and rushed on alone up to the nursery, her heart thumping in horrified anticipation of what she might find. Or rather, not find.

She burst into the nursery, scarlet-faced. There was Nurse seated beside the fire, a goffering iron in her hand and one of Susan's frilled caps upon her knee. And there was the cradle beside her, empty.

"Where's the baby gone?" cried Fanny in anguish. "What has happened to the baby?"

"No need to shout like that, Fanny," said Nurse calmly. "Where do you think the baby would have gone, child? Down to your Mamma, of course."

Fanny stood still in the middle of the nursery carpet. She stared suspiciously at Nurse (who went on goffering, so that the room was filled with the familiar nursery smell of scorched linen) and said, "I want to see it. Her. Now."

"For gracious' sake!" said Nurse irritably. "What's the matter with you? This morning you hadn't the time for so much as a look at her. Anyone would have thought you weren't best pleased to have a new little sister. You'll see her again all in good time, when Sukie brings her up again."

And, sure enough, in a few minutes there was Sukie with the baby in her arms, crooning at her as she popped her back into the cradle again, where the baby instantly set up a determined wail. Her voice, Fanny noticed, had gained strength even since this morning. Her face seemed even redder, too, and her tiny fists waved about even more vigorously. She was very ugly.

"No need to hang over her like that," said Nurse. "Go off and play now."

But Fanny could not. How could she go and play when any minute . . . when any minute she did not know quite what might happen? She sat miserably beside the cradle, and in the cradle the baby howled, and Nurse ironed and goffered and sewed, and outside in the garden Albert and Emma played quiet Sunday games.

Presently the baby stopped crying and Fanny leapt anxiously to her feet to gaze into the cradle.

"She's not breathing."

"Of course she's breathing," said Nurse crossly. "Leave her be, child. Do you want to wake her up?" She held the iron close to her cheek to test the heat, and her cheek glowed red in the firelight.

It was almost dark now. The gas lamps hissed quietly to themselves on the four walls of the nursery. Sukie drew the curtains. The baby woke up and waved its fists around, and when Fanny looked into the cradle it suddenly opened its eyes and squinted at her. It had blue eyes, like Mamma and like herself, and despite its red, wrinkled face and bald little head there was a look about it—her—of Mamma. I look like Mamma, thought Fanny, everybody says so. So this baby looks like me.

The baby gave a great sigh, just like a real person, and went to sleep again. "Dear little soul," said Nurse, rocking the cradle with her foot. "A proper little angel." Fanny's heart sank still further. Oh, she thought, in horror, what am I to do?

"Nurse," she said, "if you make a prayer, in church, can you take it back again later? If it was a prayer you didn't mean?"

"Certainly not," said Nurse. "I never heard of such a thing."

"Never?"

"And that's no kind of talk for a Sunday. Nor any other day. Get on now and do your needlework before tea."

I'll take the baby and hide it, thought Fanny recklessly. And even as she thought, she knew that it was no good. Where could you hide a howling, wriggling baby? And what, in any case, would be the point of hiding something from God, who knows everything?

And in gloom and despair, as Sunday afternoon inched onward into Sunday evening, Fanny decided to run away. I'll run away, she thought, with tears pricking her eyes, I'll run away and then at least they'll know I felt bad about it. And I won't ever know what happened, added a small, guilty voice inside her head—I won't be here so I won't ever know what happened to the baby. I'll run away and be a servant, like Nellie the kitchen maid, and Papa and Mamma will never see me again but just think sad thoughts about me. It did occur to her that, if the baby was indeed going to be whisked off to Heaven, it would not be much help to her papa and mamma to find that she had disappeared as well, but that problem just confused her. I've got to run away, she thought, there isn't anything else I can do. People in storybooks frequently ran away when things got too difficult, and Fanny could see why, now.

She slipped out of the room. Nurse and Sukie were

busy; Albert and Emma had come in from the garden and were having an argument. At least two of the Young Children were crying. Nobody saw her go. She put on her Sunday coat and hat and went out of the front door and into the street.

It was not until she reached the corner that she realized she had not thought at all about where she was going, except that she was going to find work as a kitchen maid. Nellie, the kitchen maid at home, was not much older than Fanny, and certainly no bigger or stronger. Somebody will want me, thought Fanny dolefully, everybody needs a kitchen maid. But who? And who, moreover, she realized with alarm, was there in the neighborhood who did not know her, at least by sight? Everybody in their street knew her, in the big houses that were likely to have room for a kitchen maid. And nearly everybody in most of the streets round about.

She stood on the corner, under the gas lamp, feeling very lonely and dejected. It was raining, and she had never before been out in the streets in the darkness by herself. The big houses stared coldly at her through their curtained windows, shutting her out. We have plenty of kitchen maids already, they seemed

to say, be off with you. Fanny began to feel tearful again, and just as her courage was about to leave her altogether, the church clock struck, and with its striking came inspiration. The vicarage!

The vicarage, sprawling in its big, gloomy garden beside the church, was quite the biggest house in the place. The Vicar must need kitchen maids by the dozen. And, best of all, there was very little chance that the Vicar, with his huge thick spectacles and weak blue eyes that could mistake Mamma for stout Mrs. Hancock, the grocer's wife, would recognize her. To the vicarage she would go.

The driveway to the front door of the vicarage, black with bushes and trees behind which anything might lurk, terrified her. She almost ran the last few steps and snatched at the bell rope as though at a life belt. Far away, in the depths of the vicarage, the bell rang, and presently, while Fanny quivered outside the door, footsteps came shuffling down long passages.

The door opened, not very far. Fanny had expected a servant, but there, somewhere a long way above her, for he was a tall man, as well as vastly fat, was the Vicar, peering down at her through those spectacles.

"Yes?" said Mr. Chubb.

Fanny was seized with confusion and became speechless. She gazed at Mr. Chubb, and Mr. Chubb peered back, with little blue eyes that were perhaps not quite so vague and misty as Fanny had remembered.

"Yes?" he said again.

"Please," said Fanny in a rush, "I've come to be a kitchen maid. Please will you have me for your kitchen maid? I'll work very hard," she added. "I'll work all day and I'll be very good. I'm very strong. And I don't want any money at all," she added as an afterthought.

Mr. Chubb hitched his glasses higher on his nose and stared at her. "You'd better come in," he said. He opened the door wider for Fanny to come into the hall, and closed it behind her. In the gaslight he peered at her again, harder, and said at last, "Don't I know you, little girl?"

"No," said Fanny firmly.

"You don't live near here?"

"No," said Fanny. And then she said, "I live in Edinburgh." She said this partly because she knew Edinburgh was a long way away and partly because it was one of the only places she knew of, because her aunt lived there.

"Hmmm," said Mr. Chubb. He seemed to be studying Fanny's Sunday coat and hat with some interest, and it occurred to Fanny that she was rather grandly dressed for a kitchen maid. Her everyday clothes would not have been much better, though. She gave the Vicar a faint, hopeful smile.

"Hmmm," he said again. And then, "If you've traveled all the way from Edinburgh, I would think you must be cold. You had better come into my study by the fire."

As Fanny followed him into a big room, with books all the way up the walls from top to bottom, he looked back at her over his shoulder and said, "You have had a long journey, then?"

"Two hours," said Fanny with a little more confidence. She knew that it took about two hours to go from their town to London, and supposed Edinburgh must be quite as far.

"Fancy that," said Mr. Chubb thoughtfully. He gave the fire a poke and sat down in an armchair. "Take your coat off and sit down."

They sat and looked at each other. Fanny's gaze

wavered before Mr. Chubb's blue eyes—really rather sharp blue eyes, she now saw—and she looked away in confusion.

"And what," said Mr. Chubb, "makes you think I am in need of a kitchen maid?"

"This is a very big house," said Fanny timidly. "There must be a lot of work to be done."

"Indeed there is," said Mr. Chubb. "Indeed there is." He lit his pipe and puffed out a great deal of evil-smelling smoke, through which he and Fanny observed each other.

"And for how long were you in your last position?" said Mr. Chubb.

"I beg your pardon?" said Fanny, not understanding at all.

"For how long did you work at the last house where you were employed?"

"Quite a long time," said Fanny, after a little thought.

"Ah," said Mr. Chubb, with another gust of smoke. "Your mistress would have been a Scottish lady, I take it?"

"Not particularly," said Fanny with caution.

"Indeed?" said Mr. Chubb. "You surprise me. Ladies in Edinburgh are inclined to be Scottish."

Something, Fanny realized, was going wrong with this conversation. "I expect she was sometimes," she said doubtfully.

There was a silence, during which the Vicar heaved and grunted and his pipe bubbled like a stew on the stove. He appeared to be deep in thought. "Well," he said at last. "If you are to be my kitchen maid, you had better set about your duties. Cook is visiting her sister, so you will have the kitchen to yourself."

Fanny trotted behind him down what seemed a great many dark, cold corridors until they reached the kitchen. She looked around her in dismay, not being familiar with the insides of kitchens (at home the children were always chivvied away by Cook). Mr. Chubb had turned to go out of the door.

"What shall I do?" said Fanny.

Mr. Chubb looked down at her through those thick spectacles. "Come now, my dear," he said, "I surely do not have to tell you that, if you are an experienced kitchen maid." He looked beyond Fanny

into the ill-lit scullery beyond the kitchen. "No doubt the dishes require washing."

The Vicar's footsteps grew fainter and fainter in the corridor. Fanny found a grubby apron and tied it round her waist. It would not do to soil her Sunday dress: Mamma would be most displeased (but of course she was not going to see Mamma again, so that did not really matter. Two large tears welled up at this thought). She poured some water from a jug into a basin and took the first plate from what appeared to be a small mountain of dirty, greasy crockery upon the scullery table.

Ten miserable minutes later—though it seemed much longer than that—Fanny had washed, after a fashion, three plates and a jug, and a great many tears had plopped down into the basin in front of her. Her feet were cold and her back ached. Also, she was hungry, and remembered that she had had no tea. Never before, in all her nine years, had she gone without her tea. More tears of self-pity trickled into the dirty water, checked only for a moment as the new and uncomfortable thought struck her that Nellie, the kitchen maid at home, must be doing this now too, and not just now but tomorrow and every other day.

Poor Nellie, thought Fanny. And poor me, too.

As she reached for another plate, the kitchen door opened behind her.

"Ah," said Mr. Chubb. "You are making good progress, I see." And then "Tut, tut—you have let the stove go out."

Fanny looked in alarm at the great black kitchen range. Ranges, she knew, ate coal. But where did one find coal? And how did one feed that vast, baleful object?

"You will find the coal cellar beyond the back door," said Mr. Chubb.

Fanny picked up the coal scuttle and struggled with it to the back door. She filled the scuttle with coal and then found that it was too heavy to carry, so she had to take half of the coal out again. When she got back into the kitchen, Mr. Chubb, with much wheezing and grunting, was re-lighting the stove with paper and sticks.

"Thank you," said Fanny humbly.

"It seems to me," said Mr. Chubb, "that you are as ill-acquainted with kitchen ranges as I am my-self." He peered up at her, over the top of his spectacles this time.

Fanny blushed. The Vicar was turning out to be not at all the kind of person she had expected. And furthermore, she had an uncomfortable feeling that he was not taking her absolutely seriously. Could it be that he did not believe her? That, in fact, he had seen straight through her and out the other side, as it were, with those shortsighted blue eyes of his?

"I was merely," Mr. Chubb went on, heaving himself to his feet again as the range produced a satisfactory burst of flame within, "I was merely trying to save us both from the wrath of Cook, which is second only to the wrath of God."

Fanny was startled. This sounded suspiciously like some kind of joke, though not the kind of joke Papa ever made. Papa never made jokes about God. But perhaps it was a different matter for vicars.

"What would Cook do?" she said.

"She would dismiss you instantly," said Mr. Chubb gravely. "She might," he added, "dismiss me too."

Fanny laughed.

"It is no laughing matter," said Mr. Chubb, with what Fanny felt to be mock severity (though she hastily put on a serious expression). "No laughing matter at all. Cook is a very ferocious lady."

"So is ours," said Fanny with feeling, and stopped short in horror, realizing what she had said. "I mean," she went on hastily, "the last cook I met was ferocious."

"In Edinburgh?" said Mr. Chubb.

Fanny nodded uncomfortably. She wished that she had never mentioned Edinburgh, that she had never started upon this ladder of lies. It was wicked to tell lies, of course, but she now saw that it could be inconvenient also. One thing leads to another, and before you know it there is no way of going back. She wished that she had told the Vicar the truth from the beginning, and then remembered that if she had done so he would undoubtedly have sent her straight back home. And with the thought of home, her problems raised their ugly heads again—the baby and what might or might not have happened to it, and now the new problem that she had done yet another dreadful thing in running away.

"Dear me," said Mr. Chubb. "Half-past six already. Nearly time for Evensong. Perhaps you would oblige me by making a cup of tea."

Only half-past six? The church clock had been

striking six when Fanny left her own house. Have I really been a kitchen maid for only half an hour? she thought despairingly. It had seemed more like days, weeks. . . .

"Tea," said Mr. Chubb again, and Fanny jumped. "Yes, please," she said, and then "Yes, sir," as she realized that had not been what he meant at all.

What about *my* tea? she thought, as she labored to fill the great black kettle with water and lift it onto the top of the range. A picture of the nursery at home, warm with firelight and full of the smell of muffins and toast, blotted out the Vicar's kitchen for an instant, like an image of Heaven. I am being punished, thought Fanny miserably, for being so wicked. For asking for cherry tart and clotted cream and for not loving the new baby.

She made the tea—not without some difficulty, for she had never done such a thing before and only knew what to do from years of observing Nurse and Sukie at home. Then she loaded a tray and found her way back along those long dark corridors to Mr. Chubb's study.

He was busy writing at the desk, and looked critically at the tray over an untidy pile of papers. "Very nice. Thank you. We shall have to consider making you a parlormaid."

Fanny's head was still full of her own wickedness. "No, thank you," she said, her mouth quivering as tears threatened once more. "I shall have to go on being a kitchen maid for a long time because I am so wicked."

"Is that so?" said the Vicar. He poured himself a cup of tea and went on, "You are obliged to be a kitchen maid because of your wickedness?"

"Yes," said Fanny.

"And do you suppose that all kitchen maids are wicked?"

There was a short silence. "No," said Fanny, now thoroughly muddled.

"Hmmm," said the Vicar. He took a gulp of tea, put the cup down, looked intently at Fanny and said, "Supposing you sit down and tell me all about this wickedness."

Fanny hesitated. She did not want to tell anyone, and yet knew at the same time that it would be a great relief to do so. And who better than a vicar? Vicars, after all, must be experts on wickedness.

She sat down, and told.

When she had finished, there was a pause. Mr. Chubb took off his glasses and polished them on his sleeve (which served only to make them a great deal dirtier). Then he put them back on again and said severely, "What nonsense!"

"Nonsense?" said Fanny. Nonsense was disapproved of too, at home, but it was a great deal better than wickedness.

"What nonsense," said the Vicar, "to suppose that the Almighty, having gone to all that trouble to provide a new member of your family, should decide to take her back again merely to oblige you."

"Oh," said Fanny, thoroughly abashed. Put like that the Vicar was entirely right. "But the cherry tart?" she went on anxiously. "He sent the cherry tart."

"Cherry tart is another matter altogether," said the Vicar. "A mere trifle. I beg your pardon, I mean a mere cherry tart." And his large person heaved and shook and brought forth what was undoubtedly a laugh.

Fanny felt a twinge of indignation. She did not

52

think that her affairs were anything to laugh about. She decided to abandon everything.

"And I have never been a kitchen maid," she said. "And I haven't ever been to Edinburgh. So I have told lies as well."

"My dear," said the Vicar, "I never supposed otherwise. Kitchen maids do not wear fur-trimmed Sunday coats."

"Oh," said Fanny, crestfallen.

"The same Sunday coat, indeed," said the Vicar, "that I observed in church this morning."

Fanny felt foolish, extremely foolish, but at the same time relieved of a great weight. It was the same feeling, vastly magnified, as the discovery that the cup you have just dropped is not, in fact, broken. If the Vicar did not consider her wicked, then she could not, in fact, be wicked.

"You don't think then," she said, in a small voice, "that God will take the new baby back?"

"I very much doubt if He ever considered the matter," said Mr. Chubb.

There was a silence. Fanny heaved a great sigh. If the Vicar said that, then that must be the case.

Mr. Chubb finished his tea, put the cup down, and stood up. "And now," he said, "unless you wish to continue your career as a kitchen maid . . ."

Fanny shook her head violently.

". . . I think I had better take you home. There is just time before Evensong, if I am not mistaken."

They walked together through the darkened streets, slowly because the Vicar's bad leg would not allow him to go very fast. And the slowness of the walk gave them time for what Fanny considered to be a very interesting conversation, during which the Vicar told her that he had been the youngest of a family of eleven children.

"It is much worse to be the eldest," said Fanny with conviction, and the Vicar disputed this most persuasively with accounts of the fearful things done to him by his elder brothers and sisters, till Fanny was hard put to maintain her side of the argument.

They reached the door of Fanny's house just at the point when the Vicar had finished telling the story of a famous family fight between himself and one of his brothers, so that for a moment, in Fanny's mind, he was translated from an old man in a surplice, about to conduct Evensong, into an angry small boy in knickerbockers.

"Well," said the Vicar, "good night." And he held out his hand.

"Good night," said Fanny. And then, with a small flood of doubt, "You are certain . . . quite, quite certain . . . that the baby will be there?"

"Listen," said Mr. Chubb.

And from the lighted nursery window at the top of the house, Fanny heard the noise of her newest sister wailing.

She went into the house, to be scolded for being late for tea ("And where did you get to, miss, I'd like to know—up and down the stairs Sukie's been, looking for you high and low. . . .") and to find that the muffins had been eaten by Albert. Which, such was Fanny's relief to be at home, did not send her into anything like the rage it would have done in the normal course of events.

And that, by and large, is the end of the story. What had happened, though, did have a profound effect upon Fanny's feelings both towards cherry tart and towards the new baby. She found that she could never bear to look at a cherry again, and the new baby (who was named Ethel) became her favorite among the Young Children—indeed her favorite sister. And on Sundays, after church, she and the Vicar would exchange the brief, private smiles of two people who know something that they have no intention of sharing with anyone else.